Martha S Hill

Fame's Tribute to Children

Martha S Hill

Fame's Tribute to Children

ISBN/EAN: 9783337349141

Printed in Europe, USA, Canada, Australia, Japan

Cover: Foto ©Andreas Hilbeck / pixelio.de

More available books at **www.hansebooks.com**

FAME'S
TRIBUTE TO CHILDREN

BEING A COLLECTION OF AUTOGRAPH SENTIMENTS CON-
TRIBUTED BY FAMOUS MEN AND WOMEN FOR THIS
VOLUME DONE IN FAC-SIMILE AND PUB-
LISHED FOR THE BENEFIT OF THE
CHILDREN'S HOME, OF THE
WORLD'S COLUMBIAN
EXPOSITION

CHICAGO
A. C. McCLURG AND COMPANY
1892

EXPLANATORY NOTE.

IN presenting this volume to the public, a few
words as to its origin may not be without
interest. When it was decided to erect a Children's
Building upon the Exposition grounds, the Board
of Lady Managers called for assistance in raising
the necessary funds to carry out their project.
Among the many ways and means to this end, the
idea presented itself that a volume might be com-
piled of sentiments dedicated to little children by
famous men and women, and that an additional
interest might be given it by printing these sentiments in *fac-simile*. Acting upon this idea, a circular
containing the following paragraph was printed with
the sanction and official recognition of Mrs. Palmer,
president of the Board of Lady Managers :

"We appeal to the laurel-crowned of all countries,
whose subjects will be partakers of the benefits to
be derived from the success of this undertaking, to

aid us by contributing to our volume, a verse - even a line; a sketch (be it ever so small),— a dash of the pencil or brush; some thoughts in music, if only a few chords."

This circular, accompanied by one descriptive of the Children's Building, was sent to those whose contributions were desired. The generous response which it received has made this volume possible. We acknowledge with pleasure the debt we owe those friends who have used their influence to ensure our success, as well as the famous men and women whose sentiments, wherever written, must always command the respect and admiration of all readers.

MARTHA S. HILL.

CONTENTS.

I feel like *kneeling to children*
as the future sovereigns of this
country. God bless them every
one, and keep them, as the
lives they are to live, from all
that is evil; fill their little
hearts with sunshine and their
mature lives with grace and
usefulness.

Benj Harrison

"The child was perfectly quiet now,
but not asleep — only soothed by
sweet porridge and warmth into
that wide gazing, calm which makes
us older human beings, with our
inward turmoil, feel a certain awe
in the presence of a little child,
such as we feel before some quiet
majesty or beauty in earth or sky—
before a steady glowing planet, or
a full-flowered eglantine, or the
bending trees over a silent pathway"

Melville W. Fuller,

Nov. 4, 1892.—

Wordsworth. The Excursion. Book iv.

" I have seen
"A curious child, who dwelt upon a tract
"Of inland ground, applying to his ear
"The convolutions of a smooth lipped shell;
"To which, in silence hushed, his very soul
"Listened intensely; and his countenance soon
"Brightened with joy; for from within were heard
"Murmurings, whereby the monitor expressed
"Mysterious union with its native sea."

Saml Blatchford,
Associate Justice of the
Supreme Court of the
United States.
November 2, 1892.

Nov 2. 1892

The utter helplessness
of a little child is, to
every heart, nature's
unanswerable plea
for love and care

David J Brewer

Associate Justice of
the Supreme Court
of the United States

Longfellow   To a child

"O child ! a new born denisen"
"Of life's great city! on thy head"
"The glory of the morn is shed"
"Like a celestial benison ! :"
"Here as the portal thou dost stand."
"And with thy little hand"
"Thou openest the mysterious gate"
"Into the future's undiscovered land.

Henry B. Brown.
Associate Justice
Supreme Court, United States

Douglas Jerrold
invokes a blessing in
which I would heartily
join. upon any one who
adds to the happiness of
a child — Blessed he
says "be the hand that
prepares a pleasure for a
child for there is no saying
when and where it may
bloom forth."
Washington Nov. 4. 1892
Stephen Field

"Truly, there is nothing in the world so blessed and sweet as the heritage of children."

"If I were to close among all the gifts and qualities that which, on the whole, makes life pleasantest, I should select the love of children."

John M. Harlan

Nov 1/92

" Our childhood sits,

" Our simple childhood, sit upon a throne

" That hath more power than all the elements"

L. Q. C. Lamar

"This lesson, reader, let us two divide,
never to mingle our pleasure or our pride,
with scorn of them meanest thing that feels"
Marguerite —   Do you —

Geo. Shiras Jr

I said: Until philosophers are kings, or the kings & princes of this world have the spirit & power of philosophy, and political greatness & wisdom meet in one, and those commoner natures who pursue either to the exclusion of the other are compelled to stand aside, cities will never have rest from their evils — no, nor the human race, as I believe, and then only will this our State have a possibility of life and behold the light of day.

B. Jowett

Balliol College   Oct 11. 1892

"From all this you will, doubtless,
conclude that Herrnhut does
not suit me very well, and
that the Count and I do not
always agree. It would be
more after Isoline's taste.
I like the children's dream,
as you tell it, best. We have
been dead, and laid upon
a bier; but we will, please
God, live hereafter, for the
Children and for the Christ"

The little schoolmaster Mark
p 238

Joseph Henry Shorthouse

Nay never falter: no great deed is done
By falterers who ask for certainty.
No good is certain, but the steadfast mind,
The undivided will to seek the good:
'Tis that compels the elements, and wrings
A human music from the different air."

George Eliot's Spanish Gipsy

Millicent Garrett Fawcett

O come across the hill-side, the April-month is here,
The lamb-time, the lark-time, the child-time of the year!

* * * * * * *

O come into the wide world, for you the Spring is here,
The swift clouds are sailing, the young earth carols clear.
Come happy heart to wonder,
Come eager hands to plunder
The wide world's store,
The meadow's golden glory,
The shining towers of story
On Dreamland's shore,
To reign there all the joy-time, the Spring-time of the year.

From 'An April Song.'

Margaret L. Woods.

October 13. 1892

Little Children.

.... Helpless creatures, who have never been asked if they wished for life on any terms, much less if they wished for it on .. hard conditions.
(From "Tess of the d'Urbervilles".)

Thomas Hardy.

Oct. 8. 1892

When he tried to figure to himself the
morning twilight of childhood, so as to deal
with it safely, he perceived that it was never
pitch, never arrested, that ignorance, at the
instant one touched it, was already flushing
faintly into knowledge, that there was nothing,
that at a given moment you could say a
clever child didn't know. "The Pupil" Henry James

London
October 2, 1892

Dear Miss Hill

I am delighted to be favoured with a copy of your circular describing the proposed Home for Children at the World's Fair. The idea is most charming and I feel sure your association will work it into practical form. Never before, that I know of, was such a beneficent plan devised to gladden the children and make happy the mothers. Most cordially do I wish you a full success.

Very truly yours
Justin McCarthy.

Old Johnny Grundy

Old Johnny Grundy had a Grey Mare
  Hey! Gee! Whoa!
Her legs were thin & her hide was bare
  Hey! Gee! Whoa!
And when she died she made her Will: —
" Now old Johnny Grundy has used me ill;

"Give every dog in the Town a bone,
" But to old Johnny Grundy give thou none."

The Carver came and her image made
In the Market.place where the Children played.

And the Parson preached with unction rare: —
" Good people be kind to your old Grey Mare.

" And dont you beat her or use her ill
    Hey! Gee! Whoa!
" Or else she'll leave you out of her Will "
    Hey! Gee! Whoa!

Rudyard Kipling

The Cradle

How steadfastly she'd worked at it.
How lovingly had dressed
With all her would-be-mother's wit
That little rosy nest!

How longingly she'd hung on it—
And sometimes seemed, she said,
There lay beneath its coverlet
A little sleeping head

It came at last, the tiny guest,
In dear December's frost,
That rosy nest he never pressed...
His coffin was his bed.

Austin Dobson

19 x . 92

Happy children!
how much is done
for you now-a-days,
but remember
that whilst others
are helping you
you too must learn
to save. It is
a lesson you

can joyously
leave un, but
if neglected it
may cost you
many a bitter
tears when
the glad hours

of childhood
are long passed
& gone

M J Meath

Oct 15ᵗʰ/92.

Our Children

We long for them before they
are given to us. We
love them when they come.
    We watch over them
while they are here.
    We make every endeavor
that their lives may be
full of joy.
    If they would be happy
in after years, they should
remember all this

                        J Jefferson

مرتی از نصرت ... توریک ... الدین امپراطور میرالدین شاه قاجار ...

وزیر تمام ... فخیمه امارو ... رمضان ١٣٠٣

Souvenir of His Majesty the Emperor of Persia Nasr ed Din Shah Kajar to His Excellency the Honorable Minister of the High Government of the United States. Month of Ramazan 1303. (June 1886.—

"God gave her the child,
and gave her too an
instinctive knowledge of
its nature and requirements
which no other mortal being
can possess

 Hawthorne's "Scarlet Letter."

 Your obedient servant
 Richard Mansfield

September 20. 1892.

My mother had a large
family of children, and
we all had what we
Yankees call "a very good
time." It would hap-
pen therefore, that young
mothers would come round
to consult her as to
her methods.

But she always
said, "My dear child, there

is no method— only
get along as well
as you can, every day

Throw into life the
complete unselfishness
in which she gave herself
up to her children,
and this rule will work
very well

Edward E Hale

Roxbury. Mass
Oct. 20. '92

"Even a child is known by his doings,
whether his work be pure and whether it
be right." —

Prov. xx : 11.

"Suffer the little children to come
unto me; and run not to forbid them."
(From the lips of a dying child of
nine years of age.)

John Abell D.D. N.L.Q.
Minister ... ... Church ...

Thomas Bailey Aldrich.

December.

Verses written for a Child

Each age of life has its own
world. That of the children is
not a democracy, as often in
life an absolute monarchy. And
its sovereigns are Oberon and
Titania.

Edmund Clarence Stedman

New York
Columbus Day
1892

The cure answered with a warm smile, saying:

"My boy, God is a very practical God — no, you need not write it; just listen a moment. Yes, and so when he gave us natures like this, he gave men not wives only, but brethren and sisters and companions and strangers, in order that benevolence, yes, and even self-sacrifice, — mistakenly so-called, — might have no lack of direction and occupation; and then bound the whole human family together by putting every one's happiness into some other one's hands. I see you do not understand: never mind; it will come to you little by little. It was a long time coming to me. Let us go in to supper."

Yours truly,
G. W. Cable

Northampton, Massachusetts,
September, 1892.

"You may fool a man,—
possibly, even a woman;
but you cannot fool
a child or a dog."

"The whitest soul of
man or saint,
Is black beside a
child's."

Thos Nelson Page

South Berwick.
Maine

So the Friday Club is going to open a Childrens Home? I wish that it may entertain many a young angel unawares

It seems to me that it will be a very good chance for teaching and helping some young mothers who come from lonely places and who have not been able to learn the newest ways of caring for little children and making them happy. Could not some good advice be printed in a brief and simple way after the fashion of Day Nursery rules and given to those who come for the pleased and replete babies at night? I am not sure that the babies aren't going to have the best of it at the great Enterprise!

Sarah Orne Jewett

A Child's Logic

(A true incident)

Two eyes of a purple pansy's hue,
Two eyes met mine in calm survey: —
"My child, I like your eyes so true!"
Then did the little maiden say,
"If you like my eyes, you like me, too!"

Edith M. Thomas

Divine is Infancy —
That crystal cup a-brim with potency.

Julian Hawthorne.

For the Children's Home Album
Chicago.

Il vero progresso è possibile a questa sola condi-
zione: che la nuova generazione, che viene su, val-
ga più della nostra, in rapporto all'intelletto e al
cuore. Bisogna che gli educatori abbiano sempre
presente questa verità.

Roma 23 Ottobre 1892

Pietro Blaserna

Come dobbiamo trattare i fanciulli

.... Et offerebant illi parvulos, ut tangeret
eos. Discipuli autem comminabantur offerentibus.
Quos cum videret Jesus, indigne tulit, et ait
illis: Sinite parvulos venire ad me, et ne
prohibueritis eos....... Et complexans eos, et
imponens manus super illos, benedicebat eos......

Evangelium Marci X. 13–16.

Giovanni Schiaparelli.

A beautiful voice
is the gift of God —
[signature illegible]

1892

A child's candor, simplicity
and faith would, in a man,
indicate greatness.

The door-yard gate is the dead-
line of boyhood for "Where there's
drink there's danger" and the
legalized dram shop dominates
the street. Be it our part, as
women to explore "the regions
beyond" and to play the part of
St. George against the dragon
to every enemy of childhood
outside the door-yard gate.
Then shall Society and
Government and the great World
be but a Larger Home for
little feet

Frances E. Willard

Rest Cottage, Evanston, Ill
August, 1892.

God's little ones are to become
the great of the earth. May all
who have the training of these
tender plants of the Kingdom, teach
them to cling to the Saviour and His
dear Cross as the ivy clings to the
strong oak.　Maud B. Booth

19 octobre 1892 —

Two Vallies.

I.

Yes, tis a glorious sight
This valley, that mountain height!

II.

The river's plunge and roar
Echoes the ocean shore

III.

Whatstime in waves enorm
Breaks the gigantic storm.

IV.

The wooded mount doth climb
To a thought intense, sublime.

V.

The glory of all I feel, —
But my heart, my heart will steal

VI.

Far back to the least of valleys

VII.

Where a slow brook curves and dallies, —
Where a boy, in the twilight gleam
Walks alone with his dream.

R.W.Rieder.

With Trumpet and Drum.

With big tin trumpet and little red drum,

Marching like soldiers, the children come;

It's this way and that way they circle and file —

My! but that music of theirs is fine!

This way and that way, and after a while

They march straight into this heart of mine!

A sturdy old heart, but it has to succumb

To the blare of that trumpet and beat of that drum!

Come on, little people, from cot and from hall —

This heart it hath welcome and room for you all!

It will sing you its songs and warm you with love,

As your dear little arms with my arms intertwine;

It will rock you away to the dreamland above —

Oh, a jolly old heart is this old heart of mine,

And jollier still is it bound to become

When you blow that big trumpet and beat that red drum!

To come; though I see not his dear little face

And hear not his voice in this jubilant place,

I know he were happy to bid me enshrine

His memory deep in my heart with your play —

Ah me! but a love that is sweeter than mine

Holdeth my boy in its keeping today!

And my heart it is lonely - so, little folks, come,

March in and make merry with trumpet and drum!

— Eugene Field.

Chicago, Sept 13. 1892.

The Boys

Has there any old fellow got mixed with the boys?
If there has, take him out, without making a noise.
Hang the Almanac's cheat and the Catalogue's spite!
Old Time is a liar! We're twenty to-night!

We're twenty! We're twenty! Who says we are more?
He's tipsy,—young jackanapes!—show him the door!
Gray temples at twenty?—Yes! white if we please;
Where the snow-flakes fall thickest there's nothing can freeze!

Was it snowing I spoke of? Excuse the mistake!
Look close,—you will see not a sign of a flake!
We want some new garlands for those we have shed,
And these are white roses in place of the red.

We've a trick, we young fellows, you may have been told,
Of talking (in public) as if we were old:—
That boy we call "Doctor," and this we call "Judge;"
It's a neat little fiction,—of course it's all fudge.

That fellow's the "Speaker,"—the one on the right;
"Mr. Mayor," my young one, how are you to-night?
That's our "Member of Congress," we say when we chaff;
There's the "Reverend" What's his name?—don't make me laugh.

That boy with the grave mathematical look
Made believe he had written a wonderful book,
And the Royal Society thought it was true!
So they chose him right in; a good joke it was too!

There's a boy, we pretend, with a three-decker brain,
That could harness a team with a logical chain;
When he spoke for our manhood in syllabled fire,
We called him "The Justice," but now he's "The Squire."

And there's a nice youngster of excellent pith
Fate tried to conceal him by naming him Smith,
But he shouted a song for the brave and the free,—
Just read on his medal "My country of thee"!

You hear that boy laughing?— You think he's all fun;
But the angels laugh too at the good he has done;
The children laugh loud as they troop to his call
And the poor man that knows him laughs loudest of all!

Yes, we're boys, always playing with tongue or with pen,
And I sometimes have asked,—Shall we ever be men?
Shall we always be youthful and laughing and gay
Till the last dear companion drops smiling away?

Then here's to our boyhood, its gold and its gray,—
The stars of its winter, the dews of its May!
And when we have done with our life-lasting toys,
Dear Father, take care of thy children, The Boys!

1859

Oliver Wendell Holmes.

November 10th 1892

"Doctor" Francis Thomas M.E
"Judge" George Tyler Bigelow, Chief Justice of the Supreme Court of Massachusetts
"The Speaker" Francis B. Crowninshield Speaker of the
"Mr Mayor" George W. Richardson Mayor of Newton   (House of Representatives
"Member of Congress" George Thomas Davis & Isaac Edward Holmes
"The Reverend" James Freeman Clarke and others
The "Boy with the grave mathematical look" Professor Benjamin Peirce, F.R.S. etc etc.
The "Boy with a three-decker brain" Benjamin Robbins Curtis Justice of the Supreme Court
"The nice youngster of excellent pith" Samuel Francis Smith Author "My country tis of thee". (of the United States
The "boy laughing" — previously referred to

On a dead child

Ere tears could stain thy cherub face
Or sin thy soul could leaven,
Re-enter, happy by God's grace,
Thine ante-natal Heaven.

F. W. Farrar.

All heaven, in every baby born,
All absolute of earthly heaven,
Reveals itself, though man may scorn
　　All heaven.

Yet man might feel all sin forgiven,
All grief appeased, all pain outworn,
By this one revelation given.

Soul, now forget thy burdens borne:
Heart, be thy joys now seven times seven:
Love shows in light more bright than morn
　　All heaven.

A. Swinburne

To Young Parents.

Rule your children gently while you may,
that you may be gently ruled by them when
you must.

Frederick Pollock

Man works hard over his government and his sciences and arts and in these tasks brings deep marks to his forehead but his youth and smile return when he sees happy children crossing a field of grass and flowers.

David Swing

Molto Maestro ("Dream of Jubal")

O Music highest gift to mortals known! Upon thy soaring wings
we rise above the earth, above the skies, Till open on our
ravished eyes The splendours of the Everlasting Throne!

A. C. Mackenzie

Oct. 15th. 1892

14 November 1892

They did not settle the matter that night, but soon separated for sleep. As Zury disappeared up the ladder to his roomy and airy bed-loft he called back to his father:

"Dad, I'm goin' to own a mort= gidge afore I die; mind what I say."

"Hope ye will Zury. Yew'll hev a holt of the right eend of the poker then; an' the other feller he'll hev a holt of the hot part, same as we've got naow."

"Yew bet! An' it'll sizzle his hands, tew, afore I'll ever let up on him!"

Joseph Kirkland.

I have tended six pretty cradles,
With the loveliest Babes within,
All heav'n flames of holy rapture
In a world of grief and sin.
Six babes may make six Angels.
Oh! grant it, Lord of grace,
That, lifted on their loving wings,
I too may see thy face.

Julia Ward Howe.

The Peony —

A sturdy maid:
Plump hands upon her hips,
White throat flung back,
And laughing, scarlet lips;
Full bodice, laced,
And kerchief well tucked in;
Smile for each lad —
(A kiss, perhaps, no sin!)
Plain speech — or rough —
No empty flattery —
But wholesome heart —
That is the Peony!

by Margaret Deland —

A Modest Request.

The "White City" that lies by the great inland sea,
From prow to ... was so christened by me:
And if the Chicago folks take to the name,
I want one small niche in their temple of Fame

H. C. Bunner

New York.
Puck Office,
Oct. 17/92.

The Wonder-child.

'Our little babe', each said, 'shall be
Like unto thee' - 'like unto thee!'
  'Her mother's' - 'nay, his father's' - 'eyes',
  'Dear curls like thine' - but each replies,
'As thine, all thine, & nought of me.'

What sweet solemnity to see
The little life upon thy knee,
  And whisper as so soft it lies, -
        'Our little babe!'

For, whether it be he or she,
A David or a Dorothy,
  'As mother fair', or 'father wise',
  Both when it's 'good', & when it cries,
One thing is certain, - it will be
        Our little babe .

        Richard le Gallienne .

As Little Children.

Loving and simple and sweet and dear,
Such are the guests we would summon here —
Such as the Saviour long since led
When sin-stained souls were gathered, and said —
"If you long for the grace of the undefiled,
You must become as this little child."

Louise Chandler Moulton

November — 1875.

"The baby's arms were very soft and plump, and her cheek and tangled hair were warm and moist with perspiration, and the breath that fell on Ranger's face was sweeter than anything he had ever known"

Sincerely Yours

Richard Harding Davis.

From Toilers &
Spinsters by
Anne Thackeray
            Ritchie

Boarded out children

        Loffie was a
darke faced half
wistful half tamed
little creature with
a sullen look &
then a bright one,

The story of many a
dreary tramp was
written in her face
the hardships and
troubles of other
lives than her own
   Do you see any
change in her I
asked since she
came to you? —
   Why she have all
wakened up like
said the old woman
She du sing now o'
mornings & she du
begun to curl her hair

So we understands her name is Dobbs not Stubbs They told us Stubbs at th' Union 'Tis a kindness she prated on to take Children from th' Union & larn them If Elizabeth speaks Sarce I vaey (shakin of head & other reassuring sefnals to us) Lizzie I shall take ye back Elizabeth grinned, not looking much alarmed & showed all her white teeth.

"Knowledge is now no more a fountain sealed,
Drink deep, until the habits of the slave,
The sins of emptiness, Gossip, and Spite,
and Slander die."

Mary Anderson de Navarro

London Oct. 1892.

P.T.O

It is a wonderful thing to be a child born into a world to which the boundless unfathomable love of God has been revealed; and every child so born has a right to the revelation. We, who are their grown up caretakers are responsible that they receive it, and we ought to be telling them of it, over and over, throughout every day and every hour of their young lives. Not that we are to be always preaching it, but we must be always living it in their presence, by a life of unfailing and unselfish love

and tenderness. Acts speak to a childs mind far more powerfully than words, and they will judge of the God and Father, about whom we preach to them by what they see in us. Let us see to it that we always and everywhere reveal Him as the God of love.

44 Grosvenor Road
Westminster, London
England

Hannah Whitall Smith

(Author of the Christians Secret of a Happy Life &c &c)

If the child is father,
or mother, of the man, the
Children ought to have a Home
in the Columbian Fair, so that
they will know how to treat
their grand-parents in the
greater World's Fair which it
will be their privilege to
organize.

Chas. Dudley Warner

Nov 7. 1892.

The young generation! ah, there is the child
Of our souls down the ages; to bless for it; proof
That souls we bear, with our senses filled.
  Our shuttles at thread of the woof.
  May it be braver than ours
To encounter the rattle of hostile bolts,
To look on the rising of Stranger Powers.
May it know how the mind in expansion revolts
From a nursery Past with dead letters aloof.
  (From "The Empty Purse")

George Meredith
November 1st. 1892

The assembling

of the nature of the entering

[illegible] is [crossed out] the [illegible]

[illegible] [illegible] [illegible]

all [illegible] — [illegible] their [illegible]

are [illegible] of [illegible] the [illegible]

[illegible] will be [illegible]

[illegible] [illegible].

[signature]

In the Nursery

'Where do you go, Bob, when you're fast asleep?'
'Where? O well once I went to a deep
River, farther To (is of), and a cross man said
He'd make me help, to dig, & eat black bread.
—I saw the Queen once, in her room, quite near.
She said "You rude boy Bob, how came you here?";

'Was it like mother's boudoir?'
                          Grander far
Gold chairs and things, - all over diamonds—(the!)
'You're sure it was the Queen?'
                   'Of course, a crown
Was on her, and a spangly purple gown'
'I went to heaven last-night.-
                     O Lily, no,
How could you?' 'Yes I did, they told me so,
And my best doll my favorite with the blue
Frock Jasmine, I took her to heaven too'

'What-was it like?' 'A kind of — I can't tell
A sort of orchard place, in a lone dell,
With trees all over flowers. And there were birds
Who could do talking. By soft, pretty words,
They let me stroke them & I showed it all
To Jasmine. And I heard a blue dove call
"Child this is heaven." I was not frightened when
It spoke, I said "Where are the angels then?"

'Well(?)'
So it said "Look up & you shall see—"
There were two Angels sitting in the tree,
As tall as mother; they had long gold hair
They let down the fruit they gathered there
And little Angels came for it — so sweet—
There they were beggar children in the street
And the dove said they had the prettiest things
And wore their best frocks every day.'
                                    'And wings.'

'Had they no wings?'
                'O yes & lined with white
Like swallow wings, so soft, so very light—
Fluttering about.' 'Well?' 'Well I said no—They

'So that was all' — 'They made you go away?'

147

"I did not go — but — I was gone."

"I know
But its a pity Bob. we never go
Together." "yes I have no dreams to tell
But, the next day little know in—... quite will"
"Good Bob, if I could dream you came with me
You wouldn't be there perhaps."

Perhaps — will be

Jean Tugelow.